Esther
the Kindness
Fairy

Join the **Rainbow Magic Reading Challenge!**

Read the story and collect your fairy points to climb the
Reading Rainbow at the back of the book.

This book is worth 5 points.

To Esther O'Byrne, with love

Special thanks to
Rachel Elliot

ORCHARD BOOKS

First published in Great Britain in 2016 by The Watts Publishing Group

3 5 7 9 10 8 6 4 2

© 2016 Rainbow Magic Limited.
© 2016 HIT Entertainment Limited.
Illustrations © Orchard Books 2016

A CIP catalogue record for this book is available from the British Library.

ISBN 978 1 40834 895 6

Printed and bound in Great Britain by Clays Ltd, Elcograf S.p.A

MIX
Paper from
responsible sources
FSC® C104740

The paper and board used in this book are made from wood from responsible sources

Orchard Books
An imprint of Hachette Children's Group
Part of The Watts Publishing Group Limited
Carmelite House, 50 Victoria Embankment, London EC4Y 0DZ

An Hachette UK Company
www.hachette.co.uk
www.hachettechildrens.co.uk

Esther
the Kindness
Fairy

by Daisy Meadows

ORCHARD

www.rainbowmagic.co.uk

Jack Frost's Spell

The Friendship Fairies like big smiles.
They want to spread good cheer for miles.
Those pests want people to connect,
And treat each other with respect.

I don't agree! I just don't care!
I want them all to feel despair.
And when their charms belong to me,
Each friend will be an enemy!

Contents

Start of Summer

"It's so amazing to be back on Rainspell Island again – *together!*" said Kirsty Tate, leaning out of her window and taking a deep breath of sea air.

Her best friend, Rachel Walker, clapped her hands together and bounced up and down on her tiptoes.

9

"Today is the start of the most amazing summer holiday *ever*," she said. "I'm sure of it!"

They were sharing a room at the Sunny Days Bed & Breakfast, on the island where they had first met and become best friends. They were so happy to be on holiday together there again. The girls shared a quick hug before rushing down the narrow stairs to the cosy breakfast room. Their parents were already there, poring over leaflets about things to do on the island.

"I'm sure we can find some new things to do," said Mr Walker, "even though we have visited this island so many times before."

"How about a nice long hike?" suggested Mr Tate, as the girls slipped into their seats and poured out some cereal. "It'd be interesting to explore more of the island – we all love coming to see its beautiful plants and trees."

Rachel and Kirsty shared a smile. They had an extra-special secret reason why they loved Rainspell so much. It was here that they had first become friends with the fairies!

"Hiking would be a great start to the holiday," said Mr Walker. "Let's set off after breakfast, shall we?"

"Here's an interesting leaflet," said Mrs Walker, holding out a bright yellow flyer. "It's called the Summer Friends Club."

Rachel took the leaflet and read out loud. "'A play scheme for children staying on the island. Make new friends and join in lots of fun activities.' It sounds brilliant!"

As Kirsty and Rachel were looking
at the leaflet and chattering about
the activities, the breakfast-room door
opened and Mr Holliday came in.
He ran the bed and breakfast, and he
glanced at the leaflet as he put some
toast down on the table.

"My daughter Ginny's helping to
run that club with her best friend Jen,"
he said.

Kirsty and Rachel exchanged a
special smile, wondering if Ginny and
Jen's friendship was as strong as theirs.
They knew that they were lucky to have
each other.

"Is it OK if we go to the Summer
Friends Club instead of going on the
hike?" Kirsty asked. "It sounds like lots
of fun."

"Of course," said Mr Tate. "We'll see you later and hear all about it."

"The Summer Friends Club is meeting at Rainspell Park," said Mr Holliday. "I'm sure you'll have a wonderful time."

When they had finished breakfast, the Tates and the Walkers put on their rucksacks and walking boots and set out on their hike. Rachel and Kirsty waved goodbye and then headed off towards Rainspell Park. The bed and breakfast was on a tree-lined road that overlooked the sea, and as they walked along they saw the ferry heading towards the island.

"Remember when we met on the ferry that first day?" Rachel asked, smiling at her best friend. "That was one of the best days of my life."

"Mine, too," said Kirsty. "Everything

14

I do is more fun now that I've got you to share it with – including our fairy adventures!"

The girls held hands and smiled when they saw that they were both wearing the friendship bracelets that Florence the Friendship Fairy had given them. Rainspell Island was the place where the girls had first made friends with the fairies, so it had a very special place in their hearts.

"I hope we'll meet some more fairies while we're here," said Rachel. "I love making new fairy friends."

"Fingers crossed we'll make some new human friends, too," Kirsty added. "The Summer Friends Club sounds like such a fun idea."

They reached the entrance to Rainspell Park and walked through the open gates, gazing around at colourful flowerbeds and huge old trees. The wide gravel paths were dotted with benches, and a large fountain was bubbling and splashing beside the bandstand.

"Look," said Rachel, "there's a sign for the club."

A bright yellow sign pointed them past the fountain and around a bend. They saw a large tepee-style tent in

the middle of the grass.
It was surrounded
by colourful
balloons, and
the sign next to
the tent said
'Welcome to
the Summer
Friends Club!'

Still holding hands, Rachel and Kirsty
walked into the tent. It was cool inside,
and decorated with lengths of rainbow-
coloured silk. A smiling teenage girl
hurried to greet them. She was wearing
a mint-green nametag saying 'Jen',
decorated with delicate, dark grey birds.

"Welcome to our club," she said. "Come
and join us!"

A Surprise in Goal

Peering over Jen's shoulder, Rachel and Kirsty could see another teenage girl standing at a craft table with eight other children. Jen led them over to the table and the other girl smiled at them.

"Hi girls, it's great to see you here! I'm Ginny. Right now we're all making nametags. It'd be great if everyone could introduce themselves."

The children smiled at Rachel and Kirsty and went around the table introducing themselves. Then two children called Lara and Oscar made space for the girls to join them.

"Have some felt tips," said Oscar, moving his pen pot over so they could both share it.

"I've got enough stickers for all of us," added Lara, placing her sticker sheet between them all.

"Thanks, that's so kind of you," said Rachel, with a smile.

They both took a blank nametag and started the fun of decorating.

"So is this your first time on the island?" Jen asked Rachel.

"No, we've been here lots of times," said Rachel. "It's actually where Kirsty and I first met

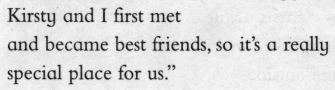

and became best friends, so it's a really special place for us."

"You're so lucky," said Lara, as she carefully drew a butterfly on her nametag. "I've been here for three days and I love it. I wish I lived here!"

"It's definitely a great place for friendship," said Ginny, exchanging a smile with Jen.

"Everyone is so nice," Kirsty whispered to Rachel. "I'm really glad we came."

As soon as the nametags were finished and the craft table was cleared away, Ginny asked everyone to come outside.

22

"We have two outdoor activities planned for today," she said. "First we'll have a game of football, and then Jen and I will challenge you all to a water-balloon fight!"

"Let's get into teams," said Jen. "I can't wait to get started!"

She divided the group into two, and Rachel and Kirsty found themselves on different teams. They grinned at each other – everyone was so friendly that they didn't mind a bit!

"All we need now are some goalposts," said Ginny. "Does anyone have anything we can use?"

Rachel pulled off her bright pink
hoodie and three of the other children
also donated colourful jumpers and
cardigans. Then the positions were agreed
and the game began. Kirsty was the
goalkeeper for her team, and she stood
in the goal with her knees bent and her
heart thumping as Rachel's team played
the ball nearer and nearer to her. She felt
nervous because she didn't play football

very often and she didn't want to let anyone down.

Lara darted across the pitch and kicked the ball as hard as she could. The ball flew towards Kirsty, who dived sideways, hands outstretched. She felt it brush her fingertips, but she couldn't quite reach it, and the first goal had been scored.

"GOAL!" yelled Rachel, jumping up and down in delight.

"Good dive, Kirsty!" called Lara.

Kirsty picked herself up and looked around at her team, feeling dreadful.

"I'm so sorry," she said. "I tried my best."

"Don't worry," said Oscar, jogging over to pat her on the back. "You tried really hard, but that was an amazing goal. Besides, it's just a bit of fun. Don't be upset!"

Everyone else on the team was smiling at her too, and Kirsty felt better at once. The game continued, and soon Oscar had scored a goal for their team. Kirsty started to really enjoy herself. Rachel

was having a good time too, running up
and down the left side of the pitch and
passing to Lara.

When Ginny blew the half-time whistle,
the score was 2–2. Rachel jogged over
to Kirsty while the others walked across
to the table of refreshments that Jen and
Ginny had prepared.

"You've made some amazing saves," said Rachel, hugging her best friend. "You're really good at goalkeeping!"

"Thanks," said Kirsty, with a grin. "You and Lara have kept me on my toes!"

"Let's go and get some juice and cookies," said Rachel. "I'm starving!"

As they walked out of the goal area, something caught Kirsty's eye. She looked down and saw that Rachel's hoodie was glowing in a very familiar and magical way.

"Rachel!" Kirsty called in a low voice. "Look!"

They knelt down beside the hoodie, which

was glowing even more brightly. The girls glanced over at the refreshments table. Everyone had their backs to the goalposts. Rachel reached out a hand and lifted a sleeve of the hoodie, and a tiny, chestnut-haired fairy fluttered out from the folds of material!

Tea in the Rose Garden

"Hello!" said the fairy in a bubbly voice. "I'm Esther the Kindness Fairy."

Her pink top was decorated with blue flowers and her matching skirt flared out as she gave a happy twirl. She had a warm, easy smile and her dark eyes shone with friendliness.

"Hello, Esther," said Rachel. "It's great to meet you."

"We always love meeting new fairies," added Kirsty, with a smile.

"I've come to invite you to Fairyland for a tea party with the Friendship Fairies," said Esther. "We've been wanting to meet you for a long time – we've heard so much about you both! Will you come? You don't need to miss a moment of the Summer Friends Club – time in the human world will stop while you're in Fairyland."

Kirsty and Rachel didn't hesitate!

"Yes, please!" they said together.

They glanced across at the other children. No one was looking their way. Esther waved

her wand and a flurry of golden sparkles surrounded the girls. They were dazzled and closed their eyes as they felt themselves shrinking to fairy size. Then gossamer wings appeared on their backs, and a wonderful scent filled the air. They opened their eyes and saw that Rainspell Park had vanished.

They were standing in a small Fairyland garden, which was filled with roses of every colour. In the centre of the garden was a white table, upon which was the most wonderful tea that the girls had ever seen. A five-tiered cake stand was filled with meringues, macaroons, eclairs

and tiny cupcakes in jewel colours. A dish was filled with bite-size triangular sandwiches, and a rose-patterned teapot steamed merrily beside matching cups and saucers.

"Welcome to our tea party!" said a chorus of tinkling voices. Three other fairies hurried to greet them, their hands outstretched.

"Let me introduce you all," said Esther. "This is Mary the Sharing Fairy, Mimi the Laughter Fairy and Clare the Caring Fairy – my fellow Friendship Fairies. It's our job to keep all friendships strong and happy."

"What a wonderful job!" said Rachel. "How do you do it?"

"With a little help from our magical objects," said Mimi, with a laugh.

Each of the four fairies took out a magical object and laid it on the white table for the girls to see. Rachel and Kirsty were enchanted to see Esther's heart brooch, Mimi's happy face pendant, Mary's yin and yang charm and Clare's mood ring. While they were examining the objects, the fairies poured out tea and filled little plates with a selection of dainty sandwiches, fondant cakes and mouth-watering appetisers. The girls couldn't resist trying a bit of everything! As they sampled the cakes and sipped tea, the fairies showed them all the different roses in the garden. Esther knew the name of each flower. They were sniffing a thornless rose called Titania, after the queen, when they heard an evil cackle. Everyone jumped and turned around.

To their horror, they saw that a ring of goblins, holding hands, had surrounded the little white table. Jack Frost was standing on top of the table, and all the delicate cakes and sandwiches were being trampled under his feet.

"Get down from there at once!" Esther demanded.

She and the other fairies darted forward, but Jack Frost hurled a bolt of blue lightning at them, and they had to dive sideways to avoid it.

Rachel and Kirsty watched helplessly as Jack Frost scooped up the fairies' magical objects and tossed them to the goblins one by one.

38

"Take these to the human world and find some friends for me," he barked at them. "I want to be super-powerful, so I need lots of friends to boss around, not just you miserable nincompoops!"

"No!" cried the girls together.

But Jack Frost and the goblins disappeared with a deafening clap of icy magic.

The fairies joined the girls, their smiles gone.

"That mean Jack Frost!" cried Rachel. "Why does he have to do such horrible things? Why can't he just go and make friends for himself, without stealing things that belong to other people?"

"He doesn't understand what friendship is," said Esther in a sad voice. "He's never been able to recognise true friendship – and now that he and his goblins have our magical objects, nobody else will have true friendship either."

"Then we have to get your objects back quickly," said Kirsty. "Let's hurry before Jack Frost spoils all friendships for ever!"

"What about *our* friendship?" asked Rachel in a quiet, worried voice. "Will we start arguing when we get back to the human world?"

Esther frowned, deep in thought. Then her gaze fell on the friendship bracelets that the girls were wearing.

"I've got an idea," she said.

She held up her wand and it started
to glow. Then she spoke, and her voice
sounded as if it were echoing around all
of Fairyland.

*"Florence, we need you! Our plans
have gone wrong.
We're inside the rose garden – please
don't be long!"*

Unkind Words

A few seconds later, Florence flew into the garden and landed beside the other fairies. They gasped out the story of what had happened, and she looked alarmed.

"Jack Frost must be stopped," she exclaimed, shaking back her blonde hair.

"Can you help to protect the girls' friendship so that they can try to get our magical objects back?" Esther asked.

Florence nodded, and asked the girls to hold up their bracelets. She pointed her wand at them and closed her eyes, and a thin spiral of rainbow-coloured fairy dust coiled out of her wand and wrapped around the girls' wrists in a figure of eight. The bracelets glowed for a moment and then Florence opened her eyes.

"I've used my 'Friends Through Thick

and Thin' spell on your bracelets," she explained. "It means that your friendship won't be affected by the loss of the magical objects, but the spell will only last for a few days. You have to find the objects soon!"

"We will," Rachel promised. "Thank you, Florence."

They hugged their fairy friends goodbye, and then Esther held their hands and whisked them back to the human world. Once again, they were kneeling down beside Rachel's pink hoodie. As usual, no time had passed while they had been gone, and the other children were still at the refreshments table. But there was no laughter or happy chatter. Instead, all Rachel and Kirsty could hear was arguing.

"Lara, you took my cookie!" Oscar was yelling. "Give it back!"

"This is your fault," Jen grumbled to Ginny. "Why didn't you buy more cookies?"

"Why didn't *you* buy any orange juice?" Ginny retorted. "It's ridiculous to only have apple juice!"

The other children were squabbling too, and Rachel and Kirsty listened in dismay as the arguments got worse. Eventually they saw Ginny hold up the palm of her hand to Jen's face.

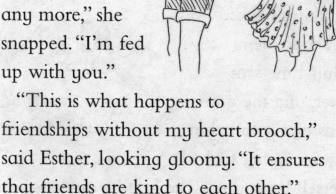

"Don't even talk to me any more," she snapped. "I'm fed up with you."

"This is what happens to friendships without my heart brooch," said Esther, looking gloomy. "It ensures that friends are kind to each other."

Kirsty's eyes filled with tears.

"Everyone is being mean and it's all Jack Frost's fault," she said. "We've got to get the Friendship Fairies' magical objects back before these friendships are ruined for ever."

"We will," said Rachel, giving her best friend a hug.

Like Kirsty, she was scared that they might lose their friendship if Jack Frost could not be stopped. Just then, the children started walking back towards them. Half-time was over, and the game was about to begin again. Esther tucked herself back inside the hoodie goalpost and the girls joined their teams.

Suddenly, a new boy in a bright green football kit ran onto the pitch. The other children gathered around him at once.

"Join our team!" called Lara.

"No, our team!" Oscar yelled. "Ignore her!"

The boy joined Lara's team, and the game began. This time, it wasn't so much fun. There were a lot of tackles, and there was even some cheating.

Ginny and Jen kept disagreeing about how to referee the match, and it seemed to drag on for ever. Then Lara got the ball and began to dribble it towards the goal.

"To me, Lara!" Rachel called. "I'm free!"

But Lara just scowled at her and passed the ball to the new boy instead. At once the other children moved out of his way – even the opposing team! He had a clear run down the pitch towards Kirsty's goal, and she got ready to stop him from scoring. He took a shot and the ball hurtled towards her. She jumped up and caught it … then let it go and made sure that it rolled between the goalposts.

"GOAL!" shouted the new boy, and Jen blew the whistle to show that it was the end of the game.

The new boy's team cheered wildly as he pulled the hem of his shirt over his head and ran around in circles. Rachel sprinted over to Kirsty.

"You dropped the ball on purpose," she said. "Why?"

Kirsty shrugged, feeling helpless.

"I have no idea," she said. "I couldn't seem to stop myself."

They looked over to where the new boy was now doing a handstand in celebration. His feet waved in the air.

"What big feet he has," said Kirsty.

"Really, *really* big," Rachel agreed.

Then they both had the same thought at exactly the same moment.

"He's a goblin!"

Esther's Brooch

Esther had heard every word, and she couldn't bear to stay hidden for a moment longer. She fluttered up from the hoodie goalpost.

"I had to come and look," she said, tucking herself under Kirsty's hair. "Where's the goblin?"

Rachel pointed to where the other children were lifting the goblin up on their shoulders, pushing and shoving each other out of the way at the same time.

Esther drew in her breath in shocked surprise.

"Look at his football shirt!" she exclaimed.

"He's wearing a brooch," said Kirsty.

"I'm sure you're not supposed to wear jewellery during a match."

"Never mind the football rules," said Rachel. "Look at the brooch!"

Kirsty narrowed her eyes and squinted, then gasped.

"It's the magical heart brooch!" she cried. "No wonder everyone is being so kind to him, and not to anyone else!"

"We'll never get it back now," said Esther, looking miserable.

"Of course we will," said Rachel in her most encouraging voice. "We've found it, so we're a huge step closer to getting it back. All we have to do is work out a plan."

Kirsty was still watching the goblin, who was boasting gleefully about his amazing goal.

"He thinks he's really good at football," she said. "That gives me an idea. Esther, could you magic up a football shirt that the goblin will think is really amazing?"

As quick as a wink, Esther waved her wand and a bright green football shirt was hanging in the air in front of Kirsty. There was a sparkly green star on the back, behind the words, 'Football Star'. Then the shirt gave a little wriggle, folded itself neatly and landed in Kirsty's outstretched arms.

"Time to suggest a swap!" said Kirsty, with a grin.

She and Rachel hurried over to join
the crowd of children. They squeezed
through the huddle until they reached
the goblin, who was now down on the
ground again.

"That was an amazing goal," said
Rachel. "Truly incredible."

"I know," said the goblin, blowing on
his fingernails and
polishing them on
his shirt.

"We've got
this shirt
for you, so
everyone can
see what a star
you are," said
Kirsty, showing
him the shirt.

"Wow, it's perfect for me!" exclaimed the goblin, his eyes widening. "Give it."

"We can only let you have it as a swap," said Rachel. "If you'll let us have your shirt as a souvenir, we'll give you this one. There isn't another one like it in the whole world."

The goblin gazed longingly at the star shirt, but then he shook his head.

"I don't want to swap," he said.

"Oh!" said Rachel. "But—"

"Get out of his way," said Oscar, pushing the girls aside. "You're crowding him!"

The girls would have tried to persuade the goblin again, but at that moment Ginny called to them from the tent.

"Time for the water-balloon fight! Come and get your balloons!" She held up a bag of balloons.

Jen snatched the bag and went to fill them with water from a tap near the fountain.

The children ran over to watch as she
made a big pile of colourful balloons.
Rachel and Kirsty followed, Kirsty
tucking the shirt into her pocket as
she went.

"Hurry up, Jen," said Ginny. "You're too
slow."

"I'm faster than *you* would be," Jen
retorted.

When the pile was finished, everyone
surged forwards, jabbing each other
with their elbows and trying to get to
the balloons first. Rachel and Kirsty
stood back and waited their turn. But
when their turn came, all the balloons
had gone. They looked at Ginny, who
shrugged.

"Tough luck," she said. "You should
have pushed in like the others."

"We really have to get that brooch back," Rachel muttered. "Everyone is being so mean!"

The water-balloon fight was already in full swing and the goblin was throwing lots, cackling as the children got wetter and wetter. But no one was throwing any balloons at him.

"The brooch is making everyone want to be kind to him," said Esther, peeking out from under Kirsty's hair.

The goblin seemed delighted that he wasn't getting wet.

"I'm the best and you're the rest!" he jeered at the other children, blowing loud raspberries and jigging about in front of them. "I'm the only one who isn't wet! I'm the quickest! I'm the greatest!"

He shrieked with laughter and hopped over to the fountain, hurling balloon after balloon at the children.

"He doesn't want to get wet," said Rachel, and a little idea popped into her mind. "If we can soak him, maybe he'll take the shirt off to get dry."

"But how can we get him wet?" asked Kirsty. "We don't have a single water balloon."

"Who needs a water balloon?" asked Rachel with a grin. "He's standing right next to the fountain!"

Forgiving Friends

The girls ducked out of sight behind
the Friends Club tent and, with a flick
of her wand, Esther turned them both
into fairies. They flew over the heads of
the other children, who were still busy
throwing water balloons at each other.
The goblin saw the fairies speeding
towards him and scowled.

"Leave me alone!" he squawked, jumping up onto the side of the fountain and flinging water balloons at them. "I know what you want, and you're not getting it!"

"The brooch doesn't belong to you!" cried Kirsty, dodging a red water balloon.

"Who cares about that?" the goblin shouted. "I love it! It makes everyone want to be my friend. Besides, I need it to bring some friends back to the Ice Castle for Jack Frost."

He had run out of water balloons now, but the fairies kept flying around his head as they replied.

"If you're kind to people, they'll want to be your friend anyway," said Esther.

"You should tell that to Jack," added Rachel.

They whizzed
around the
goblin faster
and faster, and
he started
to wobble.
Then he lost
his balance
and *SPLASH!*
He fell into the
fountain.

"Wahhh!" he wailed, pulling himself out
and falling onto the grass with a squelch.
"I'm sopping wet!"

Kirsty whispered to Esther, who waved
her wand again and returned the girls
to human size. Kirsty pulled the Football
Star shirt from her pocket, while
Rachel held out a big, fluffy towel. She

wrapped it around the goblin's shoulders
as he was wringing out his shirt, and he
cuddled it around himself.

"We could still give you this nice,
dry Football Star shirt in exchange for
Esther's magical brooch," said Kirsty.

The wet goblin looked up at her,
shivering with cold. He gazed at the dry

shirt with the sparkly star.

"Do you really think I can make friends without the magical brooch?" he asked in a small voice.

"Of course you can!" said Rachel.

"No problem!" said Kirsty.

Esther nodded, and the goblin took a deep breath.

"All right," he said.

He pulled off the wet shirt and held it out to Esther. As soon as she touched the brooch, it shrank to fairy size. The goblin pulled on the dry shirt and grinned.

"Thank you both for your kind help," said Esther, fluttering over to hover in front of Rachel and Kirsty. "I can't wait to tell the other Friendship Fairies that one of our magical objects is back where it belongs."

"I hope we'll see you
again soon," said
Rachel.

Esther blew
them a kiss,
waved and then
disappeared back
to Fairyland,
leaving a golden
shimmer in the air.

Just then, the other
children turned and waved to Rachel
and Kirsty. The goblin edged behind
Rachel's back.

"Come on," said Rachel in a kind
voice. "Come and join in."

The goblin was very shy at first, but all
the other children were being kind again,
and they welcomed him with big smiles.

"Sorry you didn't get to join in the water-balloon fight," said Oscar. "I'm afraid we've used up all the balloons."

"Never mind," said Kirsty. "We can help you to tidy up!"

Ginny and Jen made a game out of tidying up, and it wasn't long before every single burst balloon had been picked up. The goblin held the rubbish bag while the other children put the burst balloons into it.

"Thank you," said Lara, and the goblin gave her a wide grin.

"You're doing a great job," Ginny added, patting his bony head.

Jen slipped her arm through Ginny's and leaned closer.

"I'm sorry for being so grumpy earlier," she whispered.

"Me, too," Ginny replied at once. "I can't think why I was so unkind."

Kirsty and Rachel exchanged a smile when they heard this. They knew why kindness had disappeared for a while – and they were delighted to see that it had returned now that Esther had her brooch back.

When the Summer Friends Club finished for the day, the goblin scampered off to the Ice Castle. Kirsty and Rachel waved goodbye to Lara, Oscar and the others. They walked back to the Sunny Days Bed & Breakfast, and saw their parents coming back from their hike in the opposite direction.

"Did you have a good time?" asked Mrs Walker, hugging them.

"It was loads of fun," said Kirsty.

"We made some great new friends," Rachel added. "Can we go back again tomorrow?"

Their parents agreed, and the girls shared a secret smile.

"I'm looking forward to more adventures with our fairy friends, too," Kirsty whispered.

"Oh, Kirsty," said Rachel, her eyes sparkling. "That goes without saying!"

The End

**Now it's time for Kirsty and
Rachel to help...**

Mary the Sharing Fairy

Read on for a sneak peek...

"I can't wait to find out what we'll
be doing in the Summer Friends Club
today," said Kirsty Tate.

She grinned at her best friend, Rachel
Walker, who was bouncing up and down
on a space hopper. They were inside a
brightly coloured tepee tent in Rainspell
Park, where the holiday club was based.

"Whatever it is, I'm sure it'll be fun,"
said Rachel, her blonde curls flying
around her head as she bounced. "We'll
be together!"

Rachel and Kirsty had been friends
ever since their first meeting on Rainspell

Island. It was an extra-special place for them because they had also become friends with the fairies during that first holiday.

This time they were staying at the Sunny Days Bed and Breakfast with their parents. They had joined the Summer Friends Club on their first day, and were excited to find that the teenage girls who ran it, Ginny and Jen, were best friends too. Today was their second day, and they were both looking forward to finding out what Ginny and Jen had planned.

The tepee was already ringing with laughter. Oscar and Lara, who they had met the previous day, were practising one-handed cartwheels. When they collapsed to the ground, out of breath and giggling, Rachel and Kirsty came over to join them.

"Good morning!" said Lara in a cheerful voice. "It's great to see you here again. We're really looking forward to today."

"Us too," said Kirsty. "We were just wondering what we'll be doing."

"Wonder no more!" said Ginny's friendly voice behind them. "We've got something really awesome planned for today."

Read **Mary the Sharing Fairy** to find out what adventures are in store for Kirsty and Rachel!

Competition!

The Friendship Fairies have created a special
competition just for you!

Collect all four books in the Friendship Fairies series
and answer the special questions in the back of each one.

What is the name of Oscar's friend?

Lara

Once you have all four answers, take the first letter from
each one and arrange them to spell a secret word!
When you have the answer, go online and enter!

We will put all the correct entries into a draw and select
a winner to receive a special Rainbow Magic Goody Bag
featuring lots of treats for you and your fairy friends.
The winner will also feature in a new Rainbow Magic story!

Enter online now at www.rainbowmagicbooks.co.uk

Calling all parents, carers and teachers!
The Rainbow Magic fairies are here to help
your child enter the magical world of reading.
Whatever reading stage they are at, there's
a Rainbow Magic book for everyone!
Here is Lydia the Reading Fairy's guide to
supporting your child's journey at all levels.

1 Starting Out

Our Rainbow Magic Beginner Readers are perfect for first-time readers who are just beginning to develop reading skills and confidence. Approved by teachers, they contain a full range of educational levelling, as well as lively full-colour illustrations.

2 Developing Readers

Rainbow Magic Early Readers contain longer stories and wider vocabulary for building stamina and growing confidence. These are adaptations of our most popular Rainbow Magic stories, specially developed for younger readers in conjunction with an Early Years reading consultant, with full-colour illustrations.

3 Going Solo

The Rainbow Magic chapter books – a mixture of series and one-off specials – contain accessible writing to encourage your child to venture into reading independently. These highly collectible and much-loved magical stories inspire a love of reading to last a lifetime.

www.rainbowmagicbooks.co.uk

"Rainbow Magic got my daughter reading chapter books. Great sparkly covers, cute fairies and traditional stories full of magic that she found impossible to put down" – Mother of Edie (6 years)

"Florence LOVES the Rainbow Magic books. She really enjoys reading now" Mother of Florence (6 years)

The Rainbow Magic Reading Challenge

Well done, fairy friend – you have completed the book!
This book was worth 5 points.

See how far you have climbed on the **Reading Rainbow**
on the Rainbow Magic website below.

The more books you read, the more points you will get,
and the closer you will be to becoming a Fairy Princess!

How to get your Reading Rainbow
1. Cut out the coin below
2. Go to the Rainbow Magic website
3. Download and print out your poster
4. Add your coin and climb up the Reading Rainbow!

There's all this and lots more at
www.rainbowmagicbooks.co.uk

You'll find activities, competitions, stories, a special
newsletter and complete profiles of all the
Rainbow Magic fairies. Find a fairy with your name!